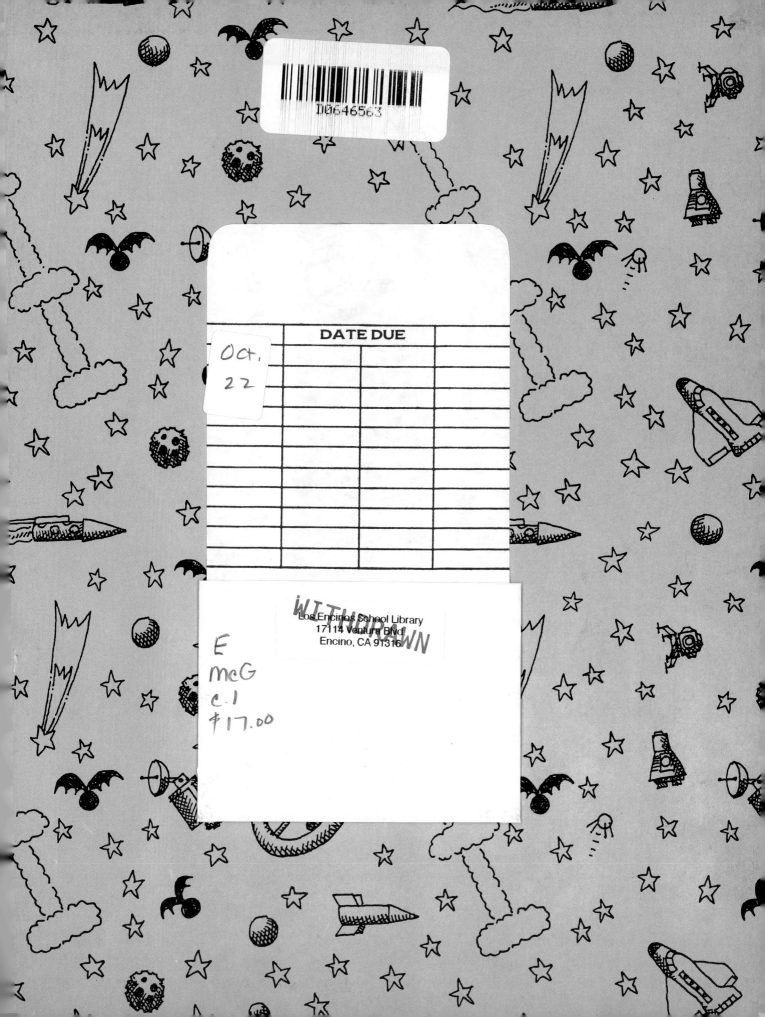

First published in the United States 1993 by
Dial Books for Young Readers
A Division of Penguin Books USA Inc.
375 Hudson Street
New York, New York 10014

Published in Great Britain 1993 by Methuen Children's Books,
a part of Reed Consumer Books
Text copyright © 1993 by Richard McGilvray
Illustrations copyright © 1993 by Alan Snow
All rights reserved
Printed in Hong Kong
First Edition
1   3   5   7   9   10   8   6   4   2

Library of Congress Cataloging in Publication Data
McGilvray, Richard, 1982–
Don't climb out of the window tonight / by Richard McGilvray ;
illustrated by Alan Snow.—1st ed.
p.   cm.
Summary: Flying ghosts and jogging giants are just two
of the ten very good reasons a little girl makes up so she won't
climb out of her window in the middle of the night.
ISBN 0-8037-1373-8
[1. Night—Fiction. 2. Bedtime—Fiction. 3. Imagination—Fiction.
4. Children's writings.]   I. Snow, Alan, ill. II. Title.
PZ7.M16767Do   1993   [E]—dc20   92-28136   CIP   AC

Don't Climb Out of the Window Tonight

by Richard McGilvraY

Illustrated by Alan Snow

Dial Books for Young Readers New York

Don't climb out of the window tonight because...

alligators are in the pond.

Don't climb out of the window tonight because...

goblins are lurking in the grass.

Don't climb out of the window tonight because . . .

ghosts are flying 'round the house.

Don't climb out of the window tonight because...

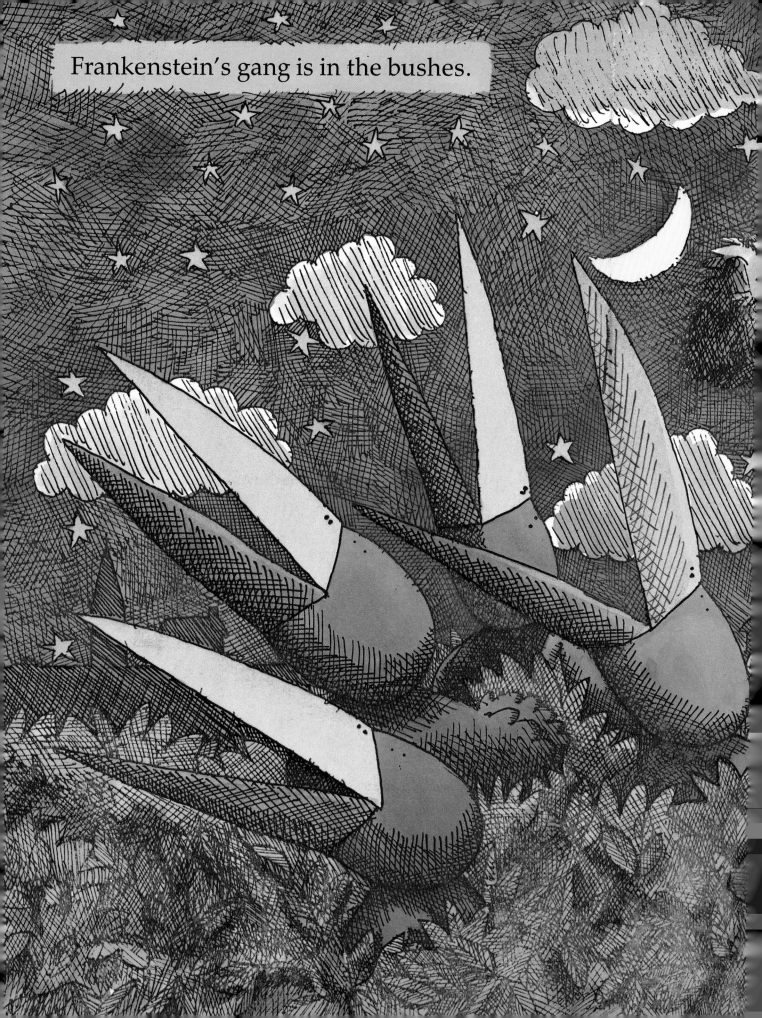

Frankenstein's gang is in the bushes.

Don't climb out of the window tonight because...

witches are hiding behind the wall.

Don't climb out of the window tonight because…

giants are jogging by.

Don't climb out of the window tonight because...

Don't climb out of the window tonight because...

dragons are in the drainpipes.

Don't climb out of the window tonight because...

bats are taking their first flying lesson.

Don't climb out of the window tonight because...

Don't climb out of the window tonight.

Wouldn't you?

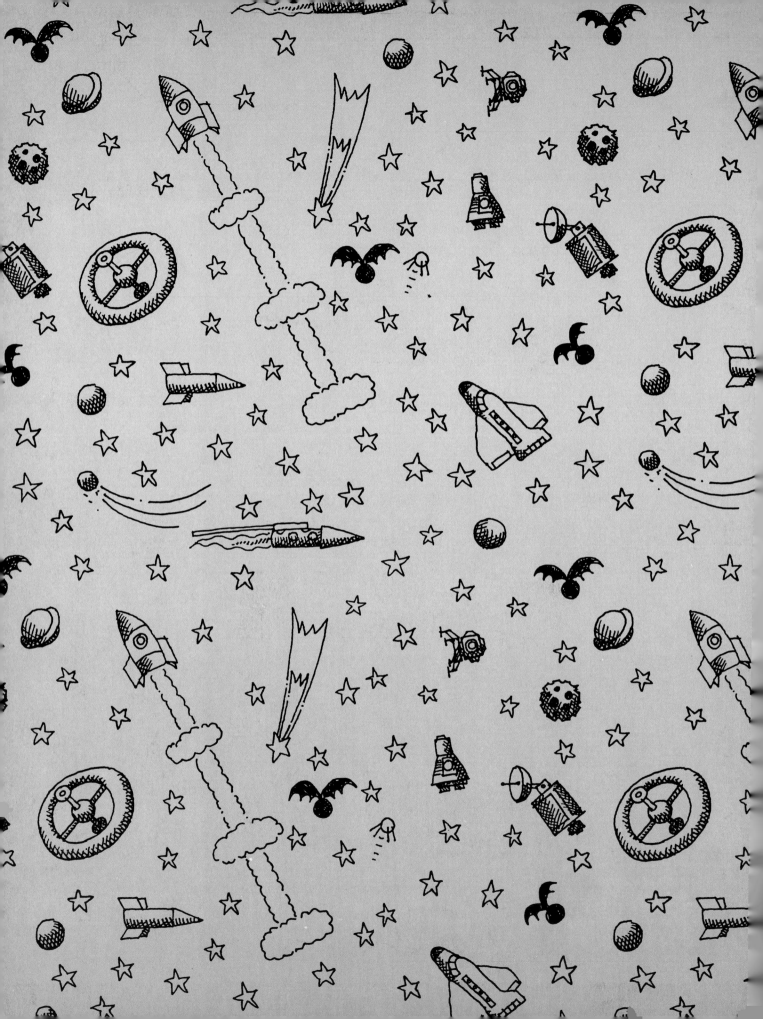